Muldoon

PAMELA DUNCAN EDWARDS

ILLUSTRATED BY

HENRY COLE

SCHOLASTIC INC.

New York Toronto London Auckland Sydney
Mexico City New Delhi Hong Kong Buenos Aires

For Geoffrey, Robert and Alistair Edwards—my men:
remembering fun times with Muldoon, Disraeli, Teague, Babushka,
Prancer, Angus, Marley, Sophie, and Mosely
—PDE

For Soozi, with love, Hen
—HE

ISBN 0-439-64068-7

Text copyright © 2002 by Pamela Duncan Edwards. Illustrations copyright © 2002 by Henry
Cole. All rights reserved. Published by Scholastic Inc., 557 Broadway, New York, NY 10012,
by arrangement with Hyperion Books for Children, an imprint of Disney Children's Book
Group, LLC. SCHOLASTIC and associated logos are trademarks and/or
registered trademarks of Scholastic Inc.

12 11 10 9 8 7 6 5 4 3 2 1   4 5 6 7 8 9/0

Printed in the U.S.A.   40

First Scholastic printing, February 2004

Muldoon works for the West family.

The Wests chose Muldoon from a lot of other applicants.

They took Muldoon
to live in their big
blue kennel.

He has a private apartment
with its own entrance so he
can come and go as he pleases.

Muldoon has great working conditions.
He gets two square meals a day,

tickles behind his ears,
and lots of tummy scratches.

Muldoon starts work early in the morning.
He's in charge of getting everyone up.

Muldoon helps Anna and Tom get dressed.
He's great at finding lost shoes.

While Anna and Tom have breakfast, Muldoon supervises so that nothing gets wasted.

He makes sure the cat stays on its diet.

When he and Mrs. West walk Anna and Tom to school,

Muldoon puts the children on a leash so they don't
run away.

Later, Muldoon helps Mrs. West put away the groceries.
He sorts through the trash to make sure she hasn't thrown
away anything valuable, by mistake.

Mrs. West realizes how hard Muldoon has been working and sends him outside for a break.

But there is so much yard work to be done.
There are holes to be dug, plants to be moved,

a lawn to be watered,

and enemies to chase.

Muldoon hardly gets a minute's rest. Before he knows it,
it's time to pick up the children and take them to the park.

Muldoon can't believe how many times the children lose their ball.

He has to find it for them over and over again.

Muldoon thinks the park is good for the children.
He helps Anna and Tom make lots of friends.

Sometimes one of them shows Muldoon a new dance.

Muldoon enjoys giving the children their bath.

But sometimes he wishes they wouldn't get him so wet, too.

Every night after supper, Muldoon offers to
wash the dishes, but Mr. and Mrs. West tell him
not to wear himself out.

When Anna and Tom are tucked into bed,
Muldoon brings their favorite book to Mr. West.
   He knows the children love it because they say,
"That one *again*, Muldoon?!"

All through the night, Muldoon keeps an ear cocked, listening for trouble.

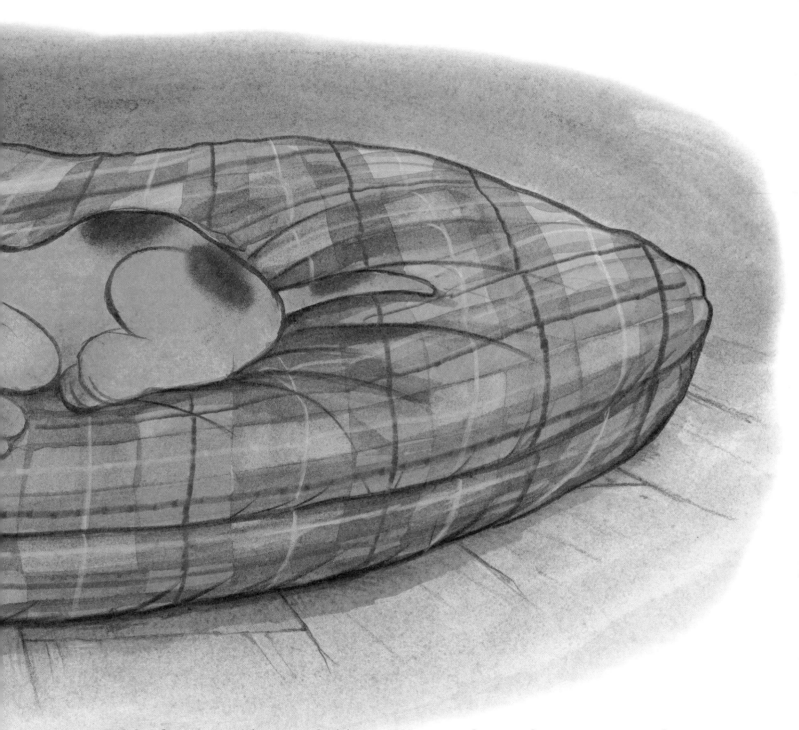

He knows Mr. and Mrs. West rely on him to guard their kennel.

Sunday

Monday

Tuesday

Muldoon thinks he has the most wonderful job in the world.

Wednesday

Thursday

Friday

But the day he likes best of all is Saturday.
Because Saturday is . . .

PAYDAY!